FLORIDA FOG PHANTOMS

Here's what readers from around the country are saying about Johnathan Rand's *AMERICAN CHILLERS:*

"I think these books are awesome!"
-Marcus L., age 11, Michigan

"I just finished THE MICHIGAN MONSTERS!
It was the best book I've ever read!"
-Stacey G., age 9, Florida

"Johnathan Rand's books are my favorite.
They're really creepy and scary!"
-Jeremy J., age 9, Illinois

"My whole class loves your books! I have two
of them and they are really, really cool."
-Katie R., age 12, California

"I never liked to read before, but now I read
all the time! The 'Chillers' series is great!"
-Lauren B., age 10, Ohio

"I love AMERICAN CHILLERS because they
are scary, but not too scary, because I don't want
to have nightmares."
-Adrian P., age 11, Maine

"I loved it when Johnathan Rand came to our
school. He was really funny. His books are great."
-Jennifer W., age 8, Michigan

"I read all of the books in the MICHIGAN CHILLERS series, and I just started the AMERICAN CHILLERS series. I really love these books!"
-Andrew K., age 13, Montana

"I have six CHILLERS books, and I have read them all three times! I hope I get more for my birthday. My sister loves them, too."
-Jaquann D., age 10, Illinois

"I just read KREEPY KLOWNS OF KALAMAZOO and it really freaked me out a lot. It was really cool!"
-Devin W., age 8, Texas

"THE MICHIGAN MEGA-MONSTERS was great! I hope you write lots more books!"
-Megan P., age 12, Kentucky

"All of my friends love your books! Will you write a book and put my name in it?"
-Michael L., age 10, Ohio

"These books are the best in the world!"
-Garrett M., age 9, Colorado

"We read your books every night. They are really scary and some of them are funny, too."
-Michael & Kristen K., Michigan

"I read THE MICHIGAN MEGA-MONSTERS in two days, and it was cool! When are you going to write one about Wisconsin?"
-John G., age 12, Wisconsin

"Johnathan Rand is my favorite author!"
-Kelly S., age 8, Michigan

"AMERICAN CHILLERS are great. I got one
for Christmas, and I loved it. Now, my sister
is reading it. When she's done, I'm going to
read it again."
-Joel F., age 13, New York

"I like the CHILLERS books because they are
fun to read. They are scary, too."
-Hannah K., age 11, Minnesota

"I read the MEGA-MONSTERS book and I
really liked it. Mr. Rand is a great writer."
-Ryan M., age 12, Arizona

"I LOVE AMERICAN CHILLERS!"
-Zachary R., age 8, Indiana

"I read your book to my little sister and
she got freaked out. I did, too!"
-Jason J., age 12, Ohio

"These books are my favorite! I love reading them!"
-Sarah N., age 10, New Jersey

"Your books are great. Please write more so I can read them.
-Dylan H., age 7, Tennessee

Look for more'American Chillers®'
from AudioCraft Publishing, Inc.,
coming soon! And don't forget to pick up
these books in Johnathan Rand's thrilling
'Michigan Chillers' series:

#1: Mayhem on Mackinac Island
#2: Terror Stalks Traverse City
#3: Poltergeists of Petoskey
#4: Aliens Attack Alpena
#5: Gargoyles of Gaylord
#6: Strange Spirits of St. Ignace
#7: Kreepy Klowns of Kalamazoo
#8: Dinosaurs Destroy Detroit
#9: Sinister Spiders of Saginaw
#10: Mackinaw City Mummies

American Chillers:
#1: The Michigan Mega-Monsters
#2: Ogres of Ohio
#3: Florida Fog Phantoms
#4: New York Ninjas
#5: Terrible Tractors of Texas
#6: Invisible Iguanas of Illinois
#7: Wisconsin Werewolves
#8: Minnesota Mall Mannequins
#9: Iron Insects Invade Indiana
#10: Missouri Madhouse
#11: Poisonous Pythons Paralyze Pennsylvania
#12: Dangerous Dolls of Delaware
and more coming soon!

AudioCraft Publishing, Inc.
PO Box 281
Topinabee Island, MI 49791

#3: Florida Fog Phantoms

Johnathan Rand

An AudioCraft Publishing, Inc. book

Graphics layout/design consultant: Chuck Beard, Straits Area Printing
Text Prep: Cindee Rocheleau, Sheri Kelley

Book warehouse and storage facilities provided by Clarence and Dorienne's Storage, Car Rental & Shuttle Service, Topinabee Island, MI

ISBN 1-893699-22-6

Printed in USA

Second Printing, November 2003

Florida
Fog
Phantoms

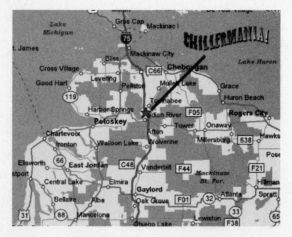

1

Before I even start to tell you this story, you have to realize something:

Florida is a cool state.

I love Florida. It's my home. I've lived here my entire twelve years.

My little sister, Maria, loves Florida.

And my Mom and Dad. We *all* love Florida.

So, when I tell you what happened to me, I'm

not doing it to scare you.

I don't want you to be frightened or afraid.

But I think you will be.

Matter of fact . . . I *know* you will.

And if you ever get a chance to come to Florida, you'll have fun. You'll have an *awesome* time.

Just beware of the fog.

Beware of the fog phantoms.

I'm not sure . . . but they *could* come back.

They might even be here now. Waiting.

Waiting . . . *for you.*

I suppose I should start at the beginning. Last summer. Right after the hurricane.

That's when weird things started to happen.

✚ ✚ ✚ ✚

We all knew there was a storm coming. We heard about it on the radio. The TV weatherman told us all about it.

It was a hurricane. You may have even heard about it or read about it, because it was the strangest storm of the year.

Not the biggest.

Not the worst.

The *strangest*.

My name is Justin Martinez, and I live in a city called Tampa. It's a city on the western side of Florida, right next to the ocean. A lot of people come here to visit, because there are a lot of things to see and do. We even have a professional football team called the Tampa Bay Buccaneers.

And Tampa happened to be in the direct path of Hurricane Alice. That's right. They give names to all of the hurricanes and tropical storms that we have, and this one they called Alice.

In 1992, a hurricane named Andrew caused twenty *billion* dollars in damage.

Hurricanes aren't anything to mess around with.

Two days before Hurricane Alice arrived, everyone in the city began boarding up their houses. Stores, shops, buildings . . . everyone boarded up their windows to protect against the high winds and heavy rains. Many people . . . including our family . . . stayed at a hotel in another city until the storm passed.

Tuesday, the storm hit just as expected. However, we were a long ways away, so we didn't have any problems.

On Wednesday, we went home. The storm hadn't damaged much, after all. It had been listed as a category 3 hurricane, which is pretty severe. However, by the time it reached land, it had dropped to a category 1, which is the lowest ranking. A category 1 can still be dangerous, though. Some of the streets around our neighborhood had been flooded, but by the time we made it home, most of the water was gone.

Everyone was thankful. A hurricane can do a lot of damage, but this time, the city was spared.

Or so I thought.

Because that night, a strange fog settled in all over the city. It was as thick as cream, and just as white. It was so thick, I could barely see the streetlight in front of our house. I had never seen fog so thick. It was kind of—

eerie.

Now, I'm twelve, and I'm not afraid of the fog.

But later that night, after I went to bed, something happened that made every single hair on my head stand straight up on end.

2

I was just about to go to bed when the phone rang. It was Caitlin McCalla, my neighbor across the street. Not only is she my neighbor, but she's also a good friend. She's really smart, too, and she helps me with my math homework.

"Have you seen Princess?" she asked. She sounded worried.

"No, I haven't," I replied. Princess is her dog.

She's a Great Dane, and she's huge.

"She ran off a little while ago. She's never done that."

"I haven't seen her," I said. "But I'm sure she'll come back."

"I hope so. I'm kind of worried about her. Can you believe this fog?"

I kept the phone pressed to my ear and looked out the window. The fog was as thick as ever. I couldn't even see any lights on in Caitlin's house across the street!

"It's really weird," I replied. "The weather guy on TV said that it was because of the storm. He says that people shouldn't drive their cars until the fog lifts."

"I'm glad the storm wasn't a real bad one," she said. "This fog is bad enough. I hope that Princess isn't—"

All of a sudden, there was a loud *click* on the line, followed by crackling static.

Caitlin was gone.

"Hello?" I spoke into the telephone. "Caitlin? Caitlin?"

No answer.

I hung up the phone and picked it back up.

There was no dial tone.

I hung up the phone again and went into the living room. Mom and Dad were watching television.

"The phone isn't working right," I said.

Dad turned. "I think it's because of the screwy weather," he replied. "It's doing some strange things all over the city."

I walked down the hall and into my bedroom. I left the light off and walked to the window.

Outside, the fog covered everything like a blanket. I tried really hard to see Caitlin's house across the street, but I couldn't. The only thing I could make out was the haunting, dim glow of the streetlight.

I yawned and climbed into bed, then I turned on the light on my nightstand. I like to read before I go to sleep. I'd been reading a ghost story, and I was almost finished with it.

I opened up the book and started to read.

The next thing I knew, the book was face down on the covers.

I had fallen asleep reading!

I closed the book and placed it on the table next to my bed, then reached up to turn the light off.

It was then that I heard a faint creaking sound.

Creeeeeeeeeak . . . .

I froze. The sound was faint, but it had been close.

Real close.

There were no other sounds in the house. It must have been late, because I didn't hear the sound of the TV on. Mom and Dad must've gone to bed.

And suddenly —

Creeeeeeeeeak . . . .

The noise sent a shiver down my spine.

Slowly, very slowly, I turned in the direction of my bedroom door. My hand still grasped the switch on the lamp, ready to turn it off.

But I wasn't turning the light off until I found out what had made that noise!

Without moving my head, I looked out the window. The fog was as thick as ever.

I looked back toward my bedroom door, and my entire body went stiff.

Creeeeeeeeak . . . .

The sound was coming from the door! My bedroom door was opening . . . *all by itself!*

I couldn't breathe.

I couldn't move.

My heart clanged in my chest.

Creeeeeeeeak . . . .

The door kept swinging open, slowly, slowly, ever so slowly . . . .

Creeeeak . . . .

I just knew that there would be some hideous

form behind my door pushing it open. It would have long fangs and claws and beady eyes.

And it was coming for me.

I knew it.

Creeeeeeeeeak . . . .

And suddenly . . . .

I could see it! I could see a small piece of something white, standing in the hall!

It was a ghost!

It was . . . it was . . . .

"Justin? Are you awake?"

My sister?!?!?!?!

I heaved a giant sigh of relief. It was only Maria. She stood in the doorway in her nightgown.

"Sorry I scared you," she said.

"Who? Me?" I replied. "I wasn't scared. Not at all."

"I am," she said, her voice quivering. "I'm scared a lot."

I looked at her. She was trembling.

"What's wrong?" I asked.

"There's . . . there's something in the fog," she said.

She glanced out my bedroom window, and I did the same.

Heavy, white mist swirled just beyond the glass. The streetlight glowed, illuminating the fog like a giant, wispy ghost.

"There's nothing in the fog," I replied. "You were having a nightmare. Go back to bed."

And with that, I turned the light off, rolled over in bed, and closed my eyes.

I heard footsteps on my bedroom floor, and then I felt Maria's hand on my shoulder. She shook me gently.

"Justin," she said, "I saw something out there in the fog. It was moving. Some kind of creature. I'm scared. I really, really am."

I rolled over and turned toward her.

"There's nothing in the fog," I insisted angrily. "Go back to bed and quit bugging me!"

She drew her hand back from my shoulder, but she didn't move. She just stood there and sniffled.

Great, I thought. *I'm going to make her cry.*

Maria is a few years younger than I am. She can be a pest sometimes, but she's pretty sweet. I guess I kind of felt bad that she was scared.

And I was making it worse for her.

I sat up, swung my legs to the floor, and stood up. I took her hand in mine.

"Listen, Maria," I said. "There's nothing in the fog. You were dreaming. I'm sure you were. Come on."

I led her by the hand, and we walked down the dark hall and into her bedroom. She climbed into bed, and I pulled the covers up to her neck. I could see the dark form of her face in the gloom.

"You're fine now," I said, and I began to walk out the door.

"Justin?" she peeped.

I stopped and turned. "What?" I asked.

"I'm thirsty," she said.

Oh, for crying out loud, I thought.

I walked down the hall, turned the corner, and went into the kitchen. The kitchen was dark, but a clock on the stove gave enough light to see.

I pulled out a plastic cup from the cupboard and filled it almost to the top, then I walked back to Maria's bedroom.

"Here's your—"

I stopped speaking.

Maria wasn't in her bed. She was standing by her window, looking out into the fog.

"I told you," she whispered, her face pressed against the glass. *"I told you there was something in the fog."*

And when I saw what it was, I gasped. I dropped the cup and it tumbled to the floor, spilling water all over the carpet and my feet.

But I didn't notice it. I just kept staring, horrified at what was in the fog beyond the bedroom window.

4.

There was something in the fog.

I could see it.

I could *feel* it.

The murky, white mist drifted like a dream beneath the streetlight.

But that wasn't the problem.

The problem was the large, blurry shape that was standing by the side of the road.

It was hard to see. The fog was so thick that I could only make out the fuzzy shape of—

Something.

What was it?

"I told you so," Maria said in a sing-song voice. She never moved, and we both kept staring at the form in the fog.

"What . . . what is it?" I managed to stammer.

Maria shook her head slowly.

"I don't know," she replied. "But I'm afraid. I don't like it."

I was afraid too, but I didn't tell Maria. I guess I didn't want her to know that I was terrified, just like she was. That would make her even *more* afraid.

I tip-toed slowly across the floor and stood next to her. My warm breath caused the glass to steam up, and I leaned back a little to keep from breathing on the window.

All the while, the strange form in the mist remained frozen, like it was staring back at us.

It was big, too. I couldn't tell for sure just how big it was, because the fog was too thick.

And then . . . *it moved.*

Maria gasped, and drew away from the window. She grasped my arm with both hands and held on tight.

"Justin . . . Justin . . . I'm scared. I'm really, really scared."

"It's . . . it's okay," I told her. I hoped that she couldn't sense the fear in my voice. "I'm . . . I'm sure that it's nothing. It's—"

The large form in the fog suddenly slunk into the shadows and disappeared.

Whatever it was, we couldn't see it anymore. It had vanished in the shadows of the unknown, where darkness slept and the beasts of the night dwelled.

And I was relieved. I didn't know what we had seen, and something told me that I didn't want to know.

Maria was still gripping my arm tightly, and we continued staring out into the fog for a long time.

Nothing.

No creature, no shape, no misty form.

Maria let go of my arm and climbed back into bed.

31

"I'm still afraid," she squeaked.

"It's gone," I told her. "Besides . . . whatever it was, it's outside. It can't get in our house."

I was wrong, of course, as I would soon find out.

I said good-night to Maria, walked to her bedroom door, and took one more quick glance out her window.

Just in case.

Just in case the form in the fog had returned.

I searched the murky mist beneath the streetlight, but I didn't see anything.

"Thanks Justin," Maria said sleepily.

I left her door open, and walked silently down the dark hall and into my bedroom.

Outside my window, the fog seemed to have gotten even thicker. I had never, ever, seen fog so thick. I've heard the expression of fog being so thick that you could cut it with a knife.

That's just what it looked like. I was certain that if I went outside with my pocketknife, I would be able to cut a square from the fog and bring it back inside.

I strode over to my window to close the drapes. I'm not saying that I was chicken or anything, but the fog was really freaking me out.

And what about that . . . that *thing* Maria and I had seen? What was it?

Was it still out there? Out there in the fog?

I stared out the window, gazing into the hazy white.

And something moved.

In the shadows.

Near the bushes by our porch. Something moved. It ducked into the shadows, like it was trying to hide from me.

My blood ran cold. My heart started

hammering again, like it had when Maria had come to my bedroom door.

What was it?

What was creeping around at night, slipping through the fog like a cat?

My breath had steamed up the window again, and I took a step back. The steam on the window faded away.

And I watched.

I looked into the shadows of the bushes. I strained my eyes to see deeper into the fog.

The creature had vanished again.

Just like before. When we were in Maria's room.

"I'm just glad I'm inside," I whispered to myself. *"I'm glad I'm inside where it can't get me."*

Whatever it is.

I breathed a sigh of relief. I was tired, and I was about to turn and climb back into my cozy bed.

It was then that I felt the icy fingers, bony and cold, wrap tightly around my neck.

My whole body tensed.

I whirled around to face a dark shape looming over me.

A voice spoke in the darkness.

"Where *what* can't get you?"

It was Dad!

Relief poured out of me like water. For a moment, I really thought that something had got me!

"Uh . . . I . . . uh . . . I thought I saw something outside. In the fog."

"I heard a noise," Dad said, "but it was inside. It sounded like something fell."

The cup of water!

I had forgotten all about it! I left the cup on the floor in Maria's bedroom!

"I dropped a cup of water in Maria's room," I replied. "But we saw something in the fog and I forgot to clean it up."

Dad looked out the window.

"What did you see?" he asked. He sounded concerned.

"I . . . I'm not really sure," I answered. "But I know I saw something. So did Maria. Honest."

Dad stepped over to the window and searched the fog. We both stood there for a moment, looking.

Watching.

Nothing in the fog moved.

"Well, maybe I should go have a look," he said. "Just to make sure everything is okay."

"And I'll go pick up the cup and clean up the

water," I said.

I followed Dad out of my bedroom. He went into the living room, and I went into Maria's room. She was already asleep. I could hear her snoring softly.

I saw the shadow of the cup on the floor, and I picked it up and walked into the kitchen. I peeled off a few paper towels from the roll, then went back to Maria's room to soak up the water that I had spilled.

After I had cleaned it up, I tossed the paper towels in the garbage and returned to my room. I walked over to the window.

Outside, in the fog, I could see Dad's form in the yard. He was carrying a flashlight, and he swept the beam back and forth. The fog was so thick that the beam of light looked like a white needle.

As Dad moved farther away, his shape vanished in the mist. I could still see the flashlight beam, but it appeared to be thinner. I watched as the blade of light swung back and forth, back and forth, searching.

And then:

I saw it.

In the street, beneath the streetlight.

A shape. *A shape in the mist.*

"Dad!" I shouted. "Behind you!"

But I was sure that Dad couldn't have heard me. After all, I was inside, and he was over at the other end of the yard.

And the form in the fog began to move.

Slowly.

Stealthily.

Like it was stalking.

Like it was preparing to attack.

"Dad!" I shouted again.

It didn't do any good. I couldn't even see my dad. All I could see was the faint beam of his light.

And the creature—the phantom in the fog—vanished.

But I knew that it was after Dad.

And what happened next was something I'll never, ever forget.

The beam of light made a sudden, quick movement.

Dad screamed.

The flashlight went out.
The phantom in the fog had attacked.

I didn't know what to do.

Dad was gone. He had screamed, and his light had gone out.

Something terrible had happened. Something awful.

There had been something in the fog, after all. It had attacked Dad.

All of a sudden, my bedroom light clicked on.

I spun around.

"What's going on?" Mom asked. She stood in the doorway, squinting in the light.

"Mom! Something got Dad! Something in the fog! I saw it! I saw it get him!"

"What are you talking about?" she asked, walking to the window. She cupped her hands around the glass like she was holding a pair of binoculars, and looked outside.

"Something happened, I tell you!" I exclaimed. "We have to help him!"

Mom hurried from my bedroom and I followed her down the hall.

Maria had heard my shouts, and she was awake, too. She was standing by her bedroom door.

"What's going on?" she asked as Mom and I rushed past.

"Dad's out there!" I said frantically. "In the fog! Something got him!"

She gasped, and her eyes grew wide.

"Stay there," I ordered.

Mom was already at the front door, and she flung it open.

Fog was everywhere. It ate up the trees and swallowed up the yard.

Dad was nowhere in sight.

"Over there!" I pointed. "That's where I heard him scream. I saw the fog creature attack him! Then his flashlight went out!"

Mom was about to call out to him, when suddenly, a shape began to take form in the creamy mist.

Dad!

Boy, was I ever glad! I thought that he was a goner, for sure!

I could hear him speaking, but he wasn't talking to me or Mom. He was talking to himself, and he didn't sound very happy.

"What happened?" Mom asked him, clicking on the outside light.

Dad stepped up onto the porch. He was wearing his striped pajamas, and he began wiping one of his slippers on the doormat.

"*This* is what's the matter!" he said angrily, raising the bottom of his slipper for us to see. "I stepped in a huge pile of dog mess! *That's* what's the matter!"

I had to fight really hard to keep from laughing. The bottom of Dad's slipper was covered with . . . well, let's just say that it was really, really gross.

I smiled, but when Dad looked up at me, I quickly closed my lips. I didn't want him to think that I was laughing at him!

But Mom wasn't smiling. She wasn't laughing. She was staring past Dad, looking into the fog.

She was staring at something.

Suddenly, I saw it, too!

There was a quick, unexpected movement, and then a form in the yard lunged forward with incredible speed.

The creature! It was attacking! *It was attacking . . . and there wasn't anything we could do!*

Mom screamed, just as the creature leapt up onto the porch. I jumped back, fearing the worst.

"Here's your creature," Dad said, stepping back.

It was Caitlin's dog, Princess!

"That's what you saw in the fog,"Dad said, pointing at the animal. "That's your creature."

Princess is a big, brown dog. She doesn't bite,

and she's very friendly. Actually, I was glad to see her. I knew how worried Caitlin was.

But Princess did a very strange thing.

Instead of sitting down on the porch or nuzzling my hand, she bounded right past me. She brushed by me, ran into our living room, turned around . . . .

And growled at us!

"Princess?" I said, backing up to the wall. She was really scaring me.

Wait a minute! I thought. *She's not growling at us! She's growling at the fog!*

Dad took off his soiled slipper and left it on the mat on the porch. He stepped inside and closed the door.

Princess stopped growling, and began wagging her stubby tail.

"What's the matter with her?" Mom asked.

Dad shook his head. "I don't know and I don't care. All I know is *that* dog made a big pile in our yard and *I* stepped in it!"

Princess looked hurt.

Dad glared at me. "And *you* can clean it up in the morning." He stormed off and went back to bed.

"Geez, it wasn't my fault," I said.

Mom smiled. She petted Princess on the head. "Come on, you," she said to the dog. "You can stay in the garage until morning. Justin, you can take Princess back to Caitlin tomorrow."

Mom put Princess in the garage, and I went back to bed. I was happy for two reasons: first of all, I was glad that Princess was safe. Caitlin would be happy, too.

But, even more importantly, I was glad that there weren't any creatures in the fog.

Unfortunately, I would soon find out otherwise.

When I woke up the next morning, the fog still hadn't lifted. It was still as thick and soupy as ever.

After breakfast, I went into the garage. Princess had been sleeping on an old blanket. She wagged her stubby tail when she saw me, and stood up.

"Come on, you," I said, reaching down to

scratch her ears. "Let's get you home."

I led the dog outside and into the fog. The mist was cold and clammy on my face.

At the edge of my driveway, I stopped. Princess stopped obediently.

I stared across the street.

"Sheesh," I said. *"I can barely see Caitlin's house."*

I rushed across the street with Princess at my side. Then I dashed across the lawn and up to the front door of Caitlin's house. I rang the doorbell.

After a minute, Caitlin's mom opened the door. Her eyes lit up when she saw Princess.

"You found her!" Mrs. McCalla exclaimed. "Caitlin will be so happy!" She turned around. "Caitlin!" she called out. "Justin is here! And he brought a friend!"

I heard the thunder of footsteps running down the stairs. Caitlin suddenly appeared. When she saw Princess, she ran up to the dog and knelt down. She threw her arms around her and gave Princess a big hug.

"Princess!" she exclaimed. "Where were you, you silly dog?!?!"

"My dad found her last night," I said, throwing my thumb over my shoulder. "In our yard. She left a . . . a *present,* and my dad stepped in it. It was kind of funny."

"Oh, I'm so glad you're home, you goofy dog." Princess licked Caitlin's cheek.

"Wanna come over and play a game?" I asked. "It's too foggy to go to the beach or the park."

"Sure," Caitlin replied. She stepped outside and closed the door behind her.

"Wow," she said, shaking her head. "This fog is really, really thick."

"I'm sure it will go away soon," I said. "Maybe then we can ride our bikes."

We walked across the yard, and stopped at the edge of the street.

Suddenly, Caitlin gasped. She grabbed my wrist and pointed.

My blood ran cold.

My skin crawled.

In front of us, in the fog, two wisping figures were coming toward us!

I held my breath as the creatures drew near.

I didn't know what to do.

Should we run? Should we turn and go back to Caitlin's house?

With every passing second, the creatures were drifting closer and closer.

There was no reason to worry, after all. A voice suddenly spoke, and I recognized who it was instantly.

"There you are," Mom said.

In the next moment, I could see her and Dad! They walked up to us and stopped. My heart slowed.

"We're going to walk down the street and visit with your grandma and grandpa," Dad said. "Stay at home and keep an eye on your sister. And don't forget to clean up that mess in the yard."

"Sorry about that," Caitlin said sheepishly. After all, it had been her dog that was responsible.

"No harm done," Mom replied. "We'll be back in a while."

And with that, they turned and began following the sidewalk. In seconds, Mom and Dad were gone, vanishing into the fog.

"Come on," I said.

We walked across the street and into our yard.

"I feel really bad that your dad stepped in the mess that Princess made," Caitlin said.

I laughed. "Actually, it was kind of funny. He sure was mad, though. I think it ruined one of his favorite slippers."

We walked into the garage and I found a shovel and a plastic bag. Then we walked out into the yard to find the pile that Dad had stepped in last night.

Now, looking back, I wonder what would have happened if we hadn't gone back into the yard. I wonder if things would have been different.

Because we were about to see something in the mist that wasn't a dog.

It wasn't Mom or Dad.

In fact, it wasn't even *human*.

And it all began when, without warning, Caitlin let out a piercing scream of terror.

When Caitlin screamed, I jumped.

"What?!?!?" I said. "What's the matter?!?!?"

Caitlin pointed into the fog. She began to back away.

I still didn't see anything."

"Over there!" Caitlin shouted.

I strained to see through the swirling, heavy mist.

And then—

I saw something move.

Something big.

"What . . . what is it?" I stuttered.

Caitlin didn't answer. Both of us remained frozen and silent, gazing into the mist.

Suddenly, a huge form was directly in front of us. It was all white, and appeared to be a part of the fog itself.

Now, I know this is going to sound crazy. You might not believe me, but this is exactly what I saw:

A Great White shark.

It was unmistakable. I've seen great whites in the shark tank at the zoo.

And that's what this was.

It seemed to swim in the air, several feet above the ground. I could see its dorsal fin, its tail, and—

Its eyes.

It was looking at us, watching us as it began to circle around.

"This . . . this can't . . . can't be happening," Caitlin stammered.

She was right. This couldn't be happening . . . but it was. Maybe the shark was a ghost or something.

Whatever it was, I wasn't dreaming. I wasn't imagining anything.

It was *real*.

And it was right in front of us.

And every time it circled, it was coming closer. It was swimming through the fog, slowly swirling around us.

Stalking us.

"We have to get back into the house," I said.

I turned and caught a glance of the garage door. It was open.

"Let's try and make it to the garage," I said to Caitlin. My voice trembled as I spoke.

Her eyes never left the huge shark. As the beast circled, we turned with it, so the creature was never behind our back.

"I can't believe I'm seeing this," Caitlin whispered. She sounded just as scared as I was.

"Believe it or not, it's here," I replied. *"And we have to get away."*

I glanced at the garage door again.

"We can make it to the garage," I said. "On the count of three we'll—"

"Justin! It's a shark! We can't outrun it! It will gobble us up in two chomps!"

The huge shark was circling closer and closer.

"Well, we have to try, or we're going to get chomped anyway," I said.

Caitlin shot a nervous glance toward the open garage door.

"And what if we don't?" she asked. "What if we don't make it?"

I gulped. I had never been so afraid in my entire life.

And I didn't have time to wonder where the shark had come from. I didn't have time to wonder how it could even be possible. I was too busy trying to figure out how we were going to get away. How we were going to get away from a fog-creature that was getting closer and closer with every passing second.

True, it was impossible. But as the saying goes, 'seeing is believing'.

And I knew what I was seeing.

A Great White shark.

Circling us . . . in our own yard!

"Okay," Caitlin finally agreed. "Let's try and make it."

The shark was moving ever closer, and now I could see its misty white teeth, long and razor-sharp. There's no mystery why the Great White is the most terrifying creature inhabiting the sea.

Or my front yard!

"Okay," I said. "On the count of three. Ready?"

"Ready," Caitlin replied.

"One," I began. The shark looked as menacing as ever.

"Two," I said, and the shark moved faster.

"Th—"

I wasn't able to finish counting. At the very second that I spoke, the Great White gave a heavy swish with its powerful tail—

and attacked!

The giant shark opened its jaws and turned toward us.

Caitlin screamed. I screamed.

Both of us, at the same time, ducked down, dropping to our knees in the damp grass. The Great White whirled above us, inches above our heads.

It had missed! Not by much, but the vicious

beast hadn't bitten us.

This time, anyway.

And I wasn't going to wait around to give the creature another chance.

I sprang to my feet and helped Caitlin up.

"Let's go! Let's go!" I shouted. I grasped Caitlin's hand and we both began to sprint toward the garage door.

"Don't look back!" I shouted. "Just keep going! We can make it!"

Our feet swished through the wet grass. It seemed like each step took a year. We weren't very far from the open garage door, but when you have some weird fog-shark attacking you, the distance seemed like ten miles!

I had to see. I had to see where the shark was. After all, if he was going to attack again, I wanted to know so we could get out of the way.

Still sprinting like mad, I snapped my head over my shoulder.

And I didn't like what I saw.

"LOOK OUT!" I screamed, pushing Caitlin to the ground. She fell forward, tumbling into the grass in a crumpled heap. I dove forward and

landed on my chest. The impact knocked the wind from me, and I rolled sideways, gasping for breath.

The shark swept past like a whirling white phantom, its gaping jaws only inches from us.

And I could almost *feel* it. I could almost *feel* the beast as it flew past.

We were in a lot of trouble. If we couldn't make it to the garage, there's no telling what would happen.

But even if we were lucky enough to make it to the garage, then what? Would the shark be able to get at us? Would he come crashing through the wall, teeth bared, gnawing and chewing and attacking?

Once again, I leapt to my feet. Caitlin was already up, and we both set off again for the door.

"Hurry!" I shouted. *"It's right behind us!"*

Somehow, I knew that if I turned to look this time, I would see the shark bearing down upon me. I knew that if I took the time to turn my head around, it would be all over for me.

For *us*.

Three more steps.

Then two.

One.

Caitlin was first to make it through the door.

I was right behind her.

Suddenly, there was a heavy tug on my shirt, and I could feel myself being pulled back.

"It's got you!" Caitlin screamed. She was standing in the doorway, her eyes huge and wide.

I reached for her, and she took my hands.

"Don't let go!" I shrieked. "Pull!"

There was a loud ripping sound as my shirt tore.

But I was free. The shark hadn't touched me. It had ripped my shirt, but it hadn't been able to get me.

I fell forward, slamming into Caitlin. We both fell to the cement floor in the garage.

Then, with a sudden burst of speed, I jumped to my feet and slammed the door closed . . . just as the shark was attacking again!

Whew! Just in time.

I was out of breath, and my heart was thrashing in my chest. Caitlin was heaving, too, breathing heavily.

"I can't believe that just happened!" she was gasping. "I can't believe it!"

I turned around and looked down at my shirt. The back of it was shredded.

"Believe it," I said. "Look at my shirt. Fog can't do that. There's something out there, Caitlin. There's something in the fog!"

She shook her head. "No," she replied. "The fog *is* something. It has become something."

Caitlin was right. The shark that had attacked us appeared to be made out of fog. It was just a large white cloud that had come alive.

How was that possible? Fog can't be alive, can it? Certainly not alive like a human being or an animal.

Could it?

Well, fog or no fog . . . that shark was *alive*.

He had attacked us, and my torn shirt was all the proof we needed.

"We've got to tell someone," I said. "Come on."

Caitlin followed me into the house. Instantly, I went to the phone and picked it up.

Still dead.

"Now what?" Caitlin asked. "Now what do we do?"

I placed my hands on my hips, and stared out the window into the back yard.

My face went white.

My jaw felt like it hit the floor.

Caitlin saw my expression of horror, and she turned to see what I was looking at.

"Oh no!" she exclaimed. Her hands flew up, covering her mouth.

Maria was outside in the fog! She was playing on her swing set . . . outside!

Maria was swinging back and forth, back and forth . . . completely unaware of any danger lurking in the fog.

"We have to get her!" I exclaimed, running to the back door. I pushed it open.

"Maria!" I shouted. "Come inside! Now!"

Maria turned to look at me.

"Huh-uh," she replied, shaking her head.

Her dark hair flung back and forth, swishing against her chubby cheeks. "Mommy said I could."

"Well, I'm in charge now, and I say get inside! Now!"

She shook her head again, and pumped herself higher into the air. I could hear the metal chain squeak as she swung herself up and down, up and down.

"Maria!" I shouted sternly, in my best older-and-wiser-big-brother voice. "Don't make me come out there and get you!"

"La, la, la, la, la," Maria sang.

She was ignoring me! She had no idea what she was doing.

"Maria! You have to come in here! There's something in the fog! It's too dangerous to be outside!"

"La, la, la, la, la-la-la," she continued singing, all the while swinging higher and higher into the air.

I decided to try another tactic.

"Maria, if you don't come here this instant, I'm going to flush your Barbie doll down the toilet!"

She turned her head. Her swinging slowed. I think the very thought of her doll getting a swirly was enough to make her stop and think twice about disobeying me.

The swing stopped. Maria stood up.

I smiled. "See," I said to Caitlin. "All you have to do is know how to push her buttons."

But Maria didn't come inside like I thought she would.

Instead, she thumbed her nose at me, turned, and began to run away! I couldn't believe it! I was only trying to help her!

"Maria Lynn!" I shouted angrily. 'Lynn' is her middle name. Sometimes, when Mom is really mad at her, she calls Maria by her first and middle names. Usually, that makes Maria stop whatever it is that she's doing.

Not today.

Not for me, anyway.

Maria ignored me, and Caitlin and I could only watch in horror as she disappeared into the fog.

But if that scared me, it was nothing compared

to the fear I felt when I saw the shape that suddenly appeared in the fog . . . .

Something that began to follow Maria!

A *panther*.

A panther had formed in the fog, and it sauntered around the swings and began to follow Maria.

However, the panther was just like the shark. It wasn't a *real* creature. It seemed to have formed right out of the mist.

That's what it was.

A mist creature.

A fog phantom.

I was more than horrified. Maria had no idea what kind of danger she was in. She had no idea that, somehow, creatures were being formed from the fog.

And she would be no match for a panther, whether it was made out of fog or not. The cat was easily bigger than her. She would be swallowed up by the big cat with one simple gulp.

"What do we do?" Caitlin asked. Her voice was tense and filled with fear.

I didn't even take time to think about it. I couldn't let that panther get Maria.

"Stay here!" I ordered Caitlin. "Stay inside!" I leapt out the back door and into the yard. Fog continued swirling about like thick, heavy smoke.

"I'm coming to help!" Caitlin shouted, following me out the door.

There was no time to argue. Any time spent arguing would be time that we needed to save Maria.

If we could save Maria.

We raced through the backyard. The panther had vanished in the fog, and there still was no sign of Maria, either.

"Maria!" I shouted as I ran. *"Where are you?"*

"You can't find me," I heard Maria pipe from somewhere in the fog. "And you can't make me come inside, either!"

I stopped running, and Caitlin did, too.

"Maria!" I called out. "You have to come inside. There are things in the fog! Dangerous things. Scary things! You have to come inside right now!"

"You can't make me!" she called out in defiance.

"Maria! Listen to me! You have to come inside the house! Now!"

There was no answer.

"Maria?" I called out.

Still no answer.

Then:

"J . . . Jus . . . Justin?" Maria peeped. Her voice sounded odd, like she was —

Scared.

"I'm right here," I said, peering into the fog.

Maria couldn't be far, but the fog was too thick to see more than a few feet in front of us.

"*There's ... there's something here,*" Maria called out. I could tell she was really scared now.

"Don't move!" I shouted out. "Just keep talking so we can find you!"

"There's . . . there's something here," she repeated. Her voice was choked with fear. She had started to cry.

"Maria ... keep talking," I said, walking in the direction of her voice. "Keep talking, so we can find you."

Suddenly, a loud snarl rang out through the fog.

Maria screamed.

The panther had attacked.

Something terrible had happened.

Something *awful.*

The panther had attacked, I was sure.

It had attacked Maria!

I ran blindly through the fog, my mind racing furiously.

Maybe it wasn't too late. Maybe, if I hurried, I could do something.

Maybe.

"Maria?" I called out.

"Maria?" Caitlin repeated. "Where are you? Are you okay?" Our voices drifted through the fog.

No answer.

And suddenly, from somewhere in the fog, I heard a snarl.

Caitlin stopped running. She grabbed my arm.

"Wait a minute!" she said.

I stopped. We listened.

A deep, menacing growl came from somewhere in the fog.

"That's not a panther," Caitlin said, taking a step toward the sound. "That's . . . that's . . . ."

I followed Caitlin as she walked slowly toward the growling beast.

Then a form came into view.

Two forms, blurred by the thick fog.

I took another step forward, ready to defend my little sister. If some freaky fog beast was going to attack her, it would have to fight me first.

But, as it turned out, I wouldn't have to fight

any phantom in the fog.

Not this time, anyway.

Maria was kneeling down in the thick grass, her arms wrapped around —

Princess!

The dog was facing us, baring her teeth, snarling and growling.

She was protecting Maria!

When Princess saw Caitlin and I, she began wagging the short stub of her tail. She stopped growling.

"Princess!" Caitlin said, rushing up to the dog. "Good girl! You're a *good* girl!" She took the dog's huge face in her hands, dropped to her knees, and hugged the animal. Princess wagged her tail so hard that her whole hind end swayed back and forth.

Maria wouldn't let go of the dog. Her arms were wrapped tightly around Princess's neck.

"Princess saved me from the big kitty," Maria said. "A big kitty came to get me, but Princess wouldn't let him." She squeezed the dog affectionately.

I looked around.

"Where . . . Where did the big kitty go, Maria?"

Still holding the dog with one arm, Maria raised her other arm and pointed.

"Over there," she said.

I turned and looked where she was pointing. The only thing I could see was creamy, thick fog.

And a pair of eyes, glaring back at us in the mist . . . .

Princess began to growl again.

We all huddled together, watching the eyes watching us.

"*Shhhhhh*," Caitlin whispered to Princess. The dog only growled louder.

"Is it the big kitty?" Maria squeaked.

"It's a big kitty, alright," I replied quietly. "It's a panther."

Panthers are Florida's state animal, but they are endangered, and you usually only see them in zoos.

And you sure don't see any that are made out of fog!

The creature in the mist was glaring at us with piercing, menacing eyes. I could see the shape of its head and its ears, but nothing else.

All the while, Princess continued snarling and growling.

Then:

The huge cat began to move.

It slunk sideways and moved toward the left, and we could see the full size of its huge body.

And, like the shark that had attacked us, the panther appeared to be made out of fog.

"What on earth is happening?" Caitlin whispered. *"How are creatures coming alive in the fog?"*

Of course, I had no answer. I was just as mystified and confused as Caitlin.

We watched the big cat as it moved, and, in the next moment, it had vanished in the mist.

We didn't move. Princess stopped growling.

We heard no sounds at all.

No birds.

No cars in the distance.

No wind.

Just—

Silence.

"We have to get inside the house," I said. "We're not safe out here."

But now we had another problem.

Which way should we go?

The only thing we could see was fog. There was nothing around us but a gray wall, and I wasn't sure exactly where our house was. I didn't even see any trees that looked familiar.

Caitlin pointed. "I think your house is that way," she said.

We waited a few more moments to see if the panther would return. There were no movements in the fog.

"Let's go," I said, taking Maria by the hand. Caitlin held on to Princess, and we all began to walk.

But something was very, very wrong.

We live in a residential area. There are houses

all around, and trees. Some people have fences in their yards.

Yet, we never saw anything.

No houses.

No trees.

No nothing.

The only thing we saw was the damp grass beneath our feet.

And fog. Lots and lots of fog.

"Something's wrong," I said, coming to a halt. "We should have found the house by now. Or we should have found someone else's house."

Caitlin looked around. "How can this be?" she asked. "How come we haven't found—"

She was interrupted by Princess's deep growls. The dog stood rigid and stiff, her hackles raised.

Princess had spotted something in the fog. Something coming our way.

And then . . . we saw it, too . . . .

17

A form slowly appeared in the mist.

It was smaller than the panther and the shark, for which I was glad. But I couldn't tell what it was.

We all huddled close together. Meanwhile, Princess continued growling and snapping. I sure was glad that she was there to protect us!

The form kept moving closer. It looked like it

was a —

"*It's a girl,*" Caitlin whispered.

And it was! It was a girl, walking slowly in the mist!

She appeared to be made out of fog, just like the shark and the panther. She had shoulder-length hair and she was wearing a dress that went just below her knees. It was so strange. I could make out her nose, her cheeks, her arms and hands . . . even her eyes.

But she was nothing but fog!

I was too afraid to move. Was she a ghost? Is that what she was? Maybe the shark and the panther were ghosts, too.

No, I thought. *There's no such thing as ghosts.*

But there's no such thing as phantoms in the fog, either!

Just then, the strange girl began to speak. Her voice sounded really strange, and there was an echo to it, like we were in a giant hall.

"*Puuuuunky,*" she called out.

Huh? What was she saying?

"*Puuunkyyyyy,*" she repeated.

"Wh . . . what's that mean?" I asked.

The girl in the mist took a step toward us, and Caitlin, Maria and I took a step back. Princess stopped growling, but the hair on her back still stood up, and she remained as alert as ever.

"Punky is my dog," she replied, her voice sounding really strange and echoing. *"I've lost Punky. I can't find him."*

"Who . . . who are you?" Caitlin asked.

I'm Amanda," the misty girl replied. *"I live here. Here in the fog."*

"You . . . you live here?" I asked. "How is that possible? Are you a ghost?"

The girl shook her head. *"No,"* she replied. *"I'm not a ghost. This cloud is my home. I live here with the other creatures in the mist."*

Talk about confused! How could a girl . . . or any creature, for that matter . . . *live in the fog?*

"But, don't you have a house?" Caitlin asked. "Don't you live somewhere?"

Again, the girl shook her head. *"No,"* she answered. *"This cloud is my home. This cloud is where I've lived for a long, long time."*

And then the girl said something that caused the blood to completely drain from my face.

"And if you don't leave the fog before it lifts, you will live here, too. Forever, and ever and ever and ever, and ever . . . ."

Forever?

Just what did she mean?

Forever.

As if the girl sensed our confusion, she began speaking again.

"There are many things that live in the cloud. Many animals, and even people. Some of us have lived here a long, long time."

"How did you get here?" I asked. "Are . . . are you a real girl?"

The strange, wisping form nodded her head. *"Yes,"* she replied. *"Many years ago, I lived here on earth. There was a hurricane, and a strange fog covered the city. My dog ran away in the fog, and I couldn't find him. Then, I lost my way. The fog plays tricks on your mind, and makes it very hard to find your way home.*

"Soon, the fog lifted, and rose up into the sky, taking me, and everything in the fog with it. I have been here ever since, looking for Punky."

Now I was *really* freaked out. I didn't want to stay in the fog forever! I don't think Caitlin and Maria did, either.

"What about the animals?" I asked. "Are they dangerous?"

"Most of them aren't," Amanda replied. *"Most of them won't hurt you. But some of them are angry. They are angry that they are trapped in the fog. They will do everything they can to make you trapped in the fog, too."*

"But how do they do that?" Caitlin asked.

"All they have to do is touch you," the girl

replied. *"If you are touched by any of us in the fog, you will become like us. You will become a phantom of the fog."*

Gulp! When I thought about how close I came to being touched by that shark, I shuddered. Lucky for me, he only touched my shirt.

"But there is someone else," Amanda continued. *"There is a mean old man who wanders the fog. He is very angry, and he knows that you're here. He knows that you're here, and he's looking for you. He wants to make you stay in the fog like the rest of us."*

"Why?" I asked.

"He is just a miserable man," the girl answered. *"You must be very careful. You must not get close to him."*

Suddenly, there was a strange barking sound from far away. It echoed through the fog. Princess started to growl.

"Punky!" Amanda cried. She turned and started off in the direction of the sound.

"Wait!" I said. "You have to tell us how . . . ."

But it was too late. Amanda, the strange, wisping fog girl, was gone.

She was gone . . . but now, there was

something else coming toward us in the fog.

And it didn't take long to realize what . . . and who . . . it was.

The old man!

Caitlin saw the figure coming, too.

So did Maria.

So did Princess. The dog began to growl and snarl like mad.

"Don't come any closer!" I ordered.

The figure in the mist stopped.

Then he took another step toward us.

"I said don't come any closer!" I repeated,

only louder this time.

The figure stopped a few feet in front of us.

It was him! It was the old man that the girl had warned us about!

Like the girl, and the other creatures in the mist, the man was made out of fog. It swirled about, forming a hat and arms and legs. I could even see deep lines in the skin on his face. His eyes were sunk deep in their sockets, and his fingers were long and bony.

"Why childrennnnn," the old man began, *"I don't wish to harm you. I don't wish to harm you at all. There's no reason to be . . .afraaaaaid . . . ."*

His voice was deep and coarse. As he spoke, he furrowed his eyebrows, and he looked scary.

"But the girl said to stay away from you," Maria said. It was the first time she had spoken in several minutes.

"Nonsenssssssssse," the old man hissed. *"I won't hurt you. I don't hurt anyone."*

"She said that you are mean, and that you want to keep us in the fog, forever, just like you."

Princess wasn't growling anymore, but she was baring her teeth angrily.

"That's because she is a very nasty little girl," the old man replied. "She is very naughty. Why, I only want to help you out of the fog."

He leaned forward, and I could see mist swirling in his eyes. He looked untrustworthy, like he was lying to us.

"Yesssssss," he continued. "I can show you how to get home. I can take you there."

"H . . . how?" Caitlin stammered.

"Very eassssssy," the old man sneered. He took a step closer. Now, he was right in front of us.

He extended his hand.

"Just take my hand, childrennnnn," he said, smiling a toothy grin. "Just take my hand and I will lead you home. I will take you there, yesssssss?"

"You're a mean old man!" Maria suddenly burst out. "You're mean and you scare me!" She began to cry.

The old man stopped.

"Why, not at all," he said. "I'm sorry to frighten you, child. I'm so sorry. Perhaps I can make it up to you . . . with a big hug!"

Without warning, the old man lunged forward, arms spread wide.

He was going to touch us! He was going to touch us, and make us stay in the fog . . . forever!

"*RUN!*" I shouted.

Caitlin ran to the left, and I grabbed Maria and ran to the right. Princess snarled and barked, but she followed Caitlin.

Whew! Just made it. The old man had nearly touched us!

"*I'll get you!*" he cried, whirling around. "*I'll get all of you! You'll all become creatures of the fog, and you'll all live here forever!"*

I held Maria's hand and ran. I can run a lot faster than her, but she was really scared and ran real fast. I had no idea where we were going, but we had to get away from the old man.

Dense fog was all around us. There were no trees, no houses, no fences. I remembered what Amanda had said about the fog trying to confuse us. She was right! As I ran, I could hardly make out the grass beneath my feet!

Behind us in the fog, I could hear the old man shouting at us. I think we made him pretty mad, but I didn't care. I sure didn't want to spend forever in some cloud!

We ran blindly through the fog, with no idea where we were going.

Finally, Maria started to get tired. We slowed to a stop, gasping for breath. I peered into the fog, thinking that, at any moment, the old man would emerge, his bony fingers reaching for us, reaching out, trying to touch us.

But he didn't.

Maria and I were alone with our pounding hearts and heaving breaths.

Alone in the fog.

"We have to find Caitlin," I told Maria after we had rested. "We have to find her, and then we have to find our way home before the fog lifts."

I had no idea where to go. No matter where we walked, we were in danger of running into the old man.

And right now, that was the last thing I wanted to do!

We walked slowly, taking small steps.

"Keep your eye out," I told Maria. "Keep your eye out for anything that moves."

As time went by, I began to get more and more worried. I knew that the fog would have to lift sometime, and soon. When we have a heavy fog in Tampa, it doesn't last too long.

But we'd never had fog like this before!

Amanda's words haunted my mind. I could hear her voice, warning us not to come in contact with any of the creatures in the fog.

If you are touched by any of us in the fog, you will become like us, she had said. *You will become a phantom of the fog.*

But Amanda didn't want to hurt us. She

wasn't trying to make us become fog phantoms. She was just trying to find her dog. I imagined that she was pretty lonely, stuck in a cloud forever, trying to find her only friend.

After Maria and I had walked for a long time, we stopped.

"This is only going to get us even more lost than we already are," I told Maria.

"I don't want to be lost," Maria whimpered.

"Don't worry," I told her. "We'll find a way out of here. I promise."

But when I saw the enormous shape suddenly loom toward us, I realized that our luck was about to run out.

Every muscle in my body went stiff. I heard Maria gasp.

Something was coming.

Not a human.

Not a panther.

And definitely not Caitlin!

Whatever was coming toward us was huge. As big as a semi truck. It was moving slow, but, it was so big, it was going to be impossible to get out of its way.

Then I noticed something.

Whatever it was, it wasn't touching the ground! It seemed to drift above the ground, coming closer and closer and closer.

And when I realized what it was, I was frozen in shock.

A whale!

It was a huge whale, coming directly for us! *In seconds, we would be devoured!*

Maria started to run, but I yanked her back.

"There's no time!" I screamed. *"We can't run fast enough to get out of its way!"*

Without another thought, I fell to the ground on my stomach, pulling Maria with me.

"Stay down!" I ordered her. *"Stay down and lay as flat as you can!"*

Our only hope was that the huge creature didn't know that we were there. If we could only lay flat enough for the whale to get by without him touching us, we might be alright.

The huge beast slowly drifted over top of us. I pressed my face to the damp grass and covered the back of my head with my hands. I could actually feel the creature as it slowly passed, only inches above us.

I knew that if I made one false move and touched the whale, it would be all over.

I tried to make myself as flat as possible. The thick, gummy odor of grass filled my nostrils, and the cool, dew-covered blades tickled my lips.

It seemed to take forever for the whale to pass. With every second, I kept waiting for something to happen. I kept waiting for the creature to brush my back or my leg or my hand.

Then it would be all over.

And then:

The whale passed. His enormous tail swished slowly, gracefully in the mist.

In another second, he was gone.

I sat up, and my relief was short-lived.

Oh, the whale was gone, alright. He had slipped away, vanishing into the mist. There was no sign of the creature at all.

But —

Maria was gone, too! Moments ago, she had been right next to me! Now, she had disappeared as quickly as the whale had.

I was alone. I was alone in the mist, and my little sister was gone.

"Maria?" I called out into the fog. My voice trembled with fear. I couldn't bear to think about what might have happened to Maria.

Had the whale eaten her? Had the beast swallowed her in one gulp? If so, how come she hadn't screamed? How come she hadn't yelled for help?

One thing I was certain of: Maria had touched

the whale. She had touched the whale, and now would forever be trapped in the cloud.

Like Amanda.

Like the panther and the shark.

And the old man.

The thought horrified me. My sister was gone.

"Maria?" I called out again. "Can you hear me?"

There was no answer. The quiet stillness of the murky gloom said all I needed to hear.

And suddenly, I became very angry. It wasn't our fault that we were trapped in the fog. We hadn't done anything wrong. This whole thing began because I took Princess back to Caitlin. It wasn't our fault at all.

With brave determination, I stormed through the grass. I didn't care about phantom sharks or panthers, or whales or an old man.

I was angry, and I was going to find my sister. And Caitlin and Princess. I didn't know how, but we were going to get out of here.

All of us.

"Maria!" I called out as I walked. "Can you

hear me?!?!"

And to my amazement, I heard a voice!

"Justin?"

It was Maria! It was Maria, and she didn't sound like she was very far away at all!

"Where are you?!?!" I shouted. "Talk to me!"

"I'm right here!" she replied, her voice closer this time.

I began moving in the direction of her voice. "Say something again so I can find you," I called out.

"What do you want me to say?" she replied.

"I don't care," I answered back. "Just keep talking. Tell me about your Barbie doll."

"But you don't like my Barbie doll!"

"I don't care! Tell me about her!"

"You said you were going to give her a swirly down the toilet!" Maria called out. "That was mean!"

I was about to say something when all of a sudden, a form began to come toward me in the fog.

I should have been happy, but I wasn't.

I was *horrified.*

I was horrified, and terribly, terribly sad.

The form coming toward me was made out of fog.

Maria had turned into a misty phantom. She would be trapped in the cold, white cloud . . . *forever*.

"M . . . Maria?" I stammered. I couldn't believe that it was her. I mean, sometimes she's a real pain in the neck. Sometimes she's a real pest.

But I was going to miss her if I couldn't see her again.

But then, if I turned into a fog creature, too, we would be together . . . but we'd never see Mom and Dad again.

Or any of my other friends.

"Maria," I said. "I'm so sorry. I should have done a better job protecting you. I'm sorry that you—"

"Sorry about what?" I heard Maria say.

Suddenly, there were *two* forms in the fog. One was . . . .

Amanda!

And right behind her was Maria . . . and she hadn't been turned into a phantom! The figure I had first spotted was Amanda, and not Maria!

I ran up to her.

"What happened?" I asked.

"I got scared of the big fish, so I rolled away in the grass. When I got up, I couldn't find you. I thought the whale ate you."

"I thought the whale ate *you*," I said. "Man, am I ever glad that you're okay."

Amanda stood close by, and she smiled. *"I found her walking alone,"* she said. *"I heard your voice and we came looking for you."*

"Thank you," I said, nodding my head. "I thought that she was a goner. Now all we have to do is find Caitlin and Princess."

Amanda turned and looked around. *"I have not seen them,"* she said. *"They could be anywhere in the fog."*

"I don't understand why we haven't seen any homes or trees or anything," I said. "I mean . . . how can that be?"

"Strange things happen in this cloud," she replied. *"Things that even I don't understand. It is possible to find your way out, but you must leave the fog before it lifts."*

"We aren't leaving without Caitlin," I said, shaking my head. "We need to find her."

Amanda agreed to help us, and we began to walk slowly through the heavy fog, searching for Caitlin and Princess. Every few seconds I would call out Caitlin's name, but there was no response.

"How do we get out of here?" I asked Amanda. "I mean . . . after we find Caitlin and Princess, then what? We've been walking and walking, and we haven't seen any houses or trees or anything. It's like we're lost in some gigantic football field or something."

"When the fog begins to lift," Amanda explained, *"you will be able to see around you.*

Houses, trees, things like that. You'll only have a minute or two to find your home and get indoors and out of the fog. If you are outside when the fog rises, then you will be taken with it — and you will become like me, and all of the other fog creatures."

There was so much more that I wanted to know about the fog. It was all so strange and weird, and I had dozens of questions.

But they would have to wait. Because there was something that Amanda hadn't told me. Something that she knew would scare the daylights out of me.

Something that even scared the daylights out of *her*.

And, as we walked cautiously through the dense, milky fog, I was about to find out what it was.

24

Suddenly, Amanda stopped walking. An expression of fear came over her face.

I stopped, and so did Maria.

"What?" I asked. "What is it?"

Amanda didn't answer. She just stood frozen, staring into the murky fog.

"What is it?" I asked again. "What's the—"

Amanda silenced me by raising a finger to her

lips. She said nothing. Maria started to say something, but I covered her mouth with my hand, then I looked at her and placed a finger to my lips, urging her to be silent. I lowered my hand from her mouth, and the three of us stood in the fog, listening.

I didn't hear a thing . . . *at first.*

And then:

Rumbling.

From deep in the ground, beneath us. The earth under our feet began to tremble and shake. I've never been through an earthquake before, but I figured that this is probably what it felt like.

Maria squeezed my hand tightly.

"What's happening?" she asked, her voice filled with fear.

"Oh no!" Amanda exclaimed. *"It's a fog wave!"*

"A what?!?!?" I asked.

"A fog wave! It's like a tidal wave, only it's a wave of fog! It will sweep us all away!"

I was a bit mystified to say the least. How could the fog sweep us away? And where would it sweep us to?

Amanda suddenly pointed. *"It's coming from*

that direction! Come on! We have to get out of its way!"

She turned and started to run. I held Maria's hand and we both began sprinting after Amanda.

"Don't look back!" Amanda called out from in front of us. *"Whatever you do, don't look back!"*

The quaking beneath my feet was really strong now, and it was becoming difficult to run.

How on earth could fog cause the ground to shake so bad? I wondered.

We continued running blindly through the fog. It was a good thing that there weren't any trees in our way, because we probably would have run into them!

The quaking grew stronger, and I felt like the ground beneath us would fall away.

Suddenly, Amanda stopped. She turned around, and her wisping, white form looked into the thick fog behind us.

"It's no use," she said. *"We can't outrun it."*

I was still really confused.

"Outrun *what?"* I asked. "Fog?"

She shook her head. *"In this cloud, we sometimes have tidal waves. They are like waves in the* ocean, except they are made from fog instead of water."

"What's the big deal about that?" I asked. "I mean . . . it's only fog. It's as light as air. What's the problem?"

"The problem is that it will sweep us all away," she replied.

"If we get touched by it, will we turn into fog?" I asked.

Amanda shook her head. *"No,"* she answered quickly. *"But there will be creatures in the wave. If you come in contact with any of them . . . well, you know what will happen."*

Gulp!

She suddenly pointed, and I realized what she was talking about.

Behind us, a huge wall of fog was building. It was four stories high . . . and it was heading right for us!

Maria screamed.

I might have screamed, too, but I don't remember. I was too shocked to remember if I did or not!

"What do we do?" I shouted to Amanda.

There was no answer from her, and when I turned . . . she was *gone!*

"Maria! Hang on tight!" I ordered. "Hang on

tight, and don't let go! No matter what!"

The enormous fog bank loomed over us, just like a tidal wave at sea. In seconds, it would be upon us.

I wasn't sure what to do. Should I hold my breath? Would the fog be like water? Could we drown? I had no answers, and Amanda was nowhere in sight. She had slipped away into the fog.

Again.

The wave rose high, up, up, higher still, growing to the size of a mountain right before us, and then came crashing down.

Instantly, Maria and I were swept off our feet. We were sent hurdling through the mist, churning and spinning. It was just like Amanda had said: the fog was like a wall of water. It picked us up and was carrying us off!

I was confused and disoriented, not knowing which way was up. I could feel Maria's tight grasp on my arm, but I couldn't see her. She had screamed for a moment when the wave had crashed into us, but now she was silent as we tumbled head over heels through the wisping fog.

Everything was a hazy gray. I couldn't see the ground, or even my own arm.

And the fog felt like water. It was thick and soupy, and as I struggled, I realized it was like swimming in a pool or the ocean.

When Amanda had said that the fog was like a tidal wave, she hadn't been kidding!

"Maria!" I shouted. "Are you all right?!?!" Even though I could still feel her tight grip, I couldn't see her.

"Yes!" she shouted. "But it's hard to hang on!"

"You have to!" I insisted. "Don't let go! Don't let go, and we'll be okay!"

I don't think I sounded very convincing, since I didn't really know what was going to happen to us.

All I knew was that if I lost hold of Maria, it would probably be the last time I ever saw her.

And I was *not* going to let that happen.

But now we had another problem.

As we tumbled and twisted through the fog, I caught a glimpse of a huge form in the mist. It was big . . . bigger than Amanda.

Bigger than the old man.

Bigger than the panther.

Maria saw it, too. She screamed.

"Justin!" she cried. *"Look out!!"*

A huge, wisping fin came into view.

And powerful jaws.

And teeth.

The Great White shark had returned. He had returned, and, while we struggled in the fog that was carrying us off, the shark seemed to have no problem swimming in the creamy, white ocean. He moved with ease through the mist . . . and he was coming toward us!

26

I had always thought that my life had been kind of boring . . . until now. Now, I had more action and adventure than I could handle!

Maria and I were on a collision course with the shark. I struggled to move and flailed my free arm in swimming motions, trying desperately to get out of the path of the stalking shark. I was certain that it was the same one that had attacked us earlier.

And something told me that, this time, he was not going to let us get away so easily.

Closer. Faster.

The shark was almost upon us. I could see his razor-sharp teeth in his mouth. Even though I knew that he was made of fog, it didn't make the beast any less dangerous. In two seconds, we would be fish food.

Suddenly, I felt something grasp my ankle. It yanked me with such force that I lost my breath. I was tugged away, in a different direction.

The shark disappeared. I didn't know if he was still around or not, but I could no longer see him.

And what was worse . . . something had a hold so tight on my ankle that I thought my foot was going to be pulled off!

"Justin!" I heard Maria shout. "Is that you?!?!"

"Of course it's—" But I didn't finish my sentence.

That voice! That wasn't Maria! That was—

Caitlin!

"Caitlin!" I cried. "Is that you?!?!"

"Yes!" I heard her shout.

She had saved us! Caitlin had saved us from the Great White shark!

In the next instant, I saw her. She was standing on the ground, but white fog was washing all around her like water. It was as if she was wading in a river of mist.

Maria and I sort of splashed down next to her. I pulled my sister to her feet and held her up in the air, above the watery fog.

"How did you . . . what did you do?" I stammered.

"I was looking for you and Maria," she said. "I got picked up by that wave of fog and landed here. I saw you and Maria tumbling above me. Boy, did you guys look weird, tumbling through the fog like that."

"Did you see the shark?" I asked.

A puzzled look came over Caitlin's face. "Shark?" she said, shaking her head. "No. I didn't see any shark at all."

"Man, you saved us just in the nick of time!" I exclaimed. "It was just about to have us for lunch, until you pulled us away. Another two seconds, and we would have been history."

The wave of fog seemed to be thinning. Oh, the creamy, gray cloud around us was just as dense as ever, but the water-like mist that churned about us was drifting off.

We had survived. We had made it through the tidal wave of fog.

And we had found Caitlin! I had never been so happy in my life.

Now, all we had to do was find Princess. Find Princess, and get out of here. Get out of the fog and into our house, wherever that was.

But now there was something else to worry about.

Something that had been washed in by the wall of fog.

And when Caitlin let out a shriek of terror, I knew that our nightmare was far from over.

Our nightmare was just beginning.

Caitlin's piercing cry rang through the fog. I spun around instantly . . . and found myself nose-to-nose . . . *with a Portuguese man-o-war.*

Now, if you ever come to Florida, here's a warning:

Watch out for the Portuguese man-o-war. It's a relative of the jellyfish family. In fact, that's what it looks like. Man-o-wars look like air-filled blob-like bubbles that float on the surface of the water. Most of them aren't very big . . . about the size of a volleyball.

It's the tentacles you have to worry about. The tentacles of the Portuguese man-o-war can be as long as thirty feet, and if you get stung, you're in deep trouble. The venom from the tentacles is very poisonous, and the stings are really painful.

Oh, they're easily avoidable. You might see them washed up near shore from time to time, if the wind has blown them from deeper water.

You just stay away from them, that's all. That's the best thing to do.

Our problem was that *this* man-o-war was made out of fog . . . and its dangerous tentacles dangled only inches above our heads!

"Hit the deck!" I screamed. Maria, Caitlin, and I fell to the ground.

"Roll! Roll! Roll!" I commanded. We started rolling away in the wet grass.

Above us, hundreds of tentacles twisted like snakes, weaving all around and back and forth, searching for prey.

"Keep rolling!" I said, as I twisted through the grass. *"Don't stop to look! Just keep rolling!"*

Suddenly, I bumped into something, and rolled over it. I heard a grunt and a groan.

"Ouch!" Maria cried. "You just ran over me, you big goof!"

I stopped rolling and quickly glanced back.

The man-o-war was nowhere in sight. Oh, I was sure that it wasn't too far away, and we'd have to be careful.

But for the time being, we were safe.

Maria bounded to her feet, and Caitlin stood up, too.

"We have to be more careful," I said. "There are things all around in this fog. We have to be on the lookout for anything."

"Including Princess," Caitlin said. She sounded worried, and I was too. I wanted to find Princess and go home. Get out of this fog, and go home.

It was not going to be easy, as we were about to find out . . . because, in the excitement of the wave and the whale and the man-o-war, I had forgotten about the old man.

We stood, unmoving. Three lone figures in the fog.

Three very *lost* lone figures.

"We're running out of time," I said. "We have to get out of the fog before it lifts."

"Not before we find Princess," Caitlin stated. I could tell that she wasn't going anywhere without her dog.

And I couldn't blame her.

But what if we didn't find Princess? What then?

Then, all of us would be trapped in the fog. We wouldn't have even had the chance to say good-bye to our parents or our friends.

We started to walk. Of course, we had no idea where we were going, but we had to do *something*. We would be wasting valuable time if we just stood there.

I told Caitlin what Amanda had told me about the fog. That when it begins to lift, we will be able to see houses and trees all around, even though we can't see them right now. We would only have a few moments to get in out of the fog, or else be trapped forever.

It sure felt strange, knowing that we were in another world . . . yet, all the while, we weren't far from our homes at all. We were so close . . . yet, so very, very far away.

We walked in silence, all the while on the look out for more creatures in the fog, when suddenly—

A dog barked!

132

We stopped.

The dog barked again. It was far away, but there was no mistake. It was a dog, alright.

"Princess!" Caitlin shouted. "Princess! Where are you?!?!?"

More barking.

"She's over there!" I heard Caitlin shout. She pointed into the fog. "She's over there somewhere!"

She began running in the direction of the sound.

"Caitlin!" I shouted. "Slow down! Stay with us!"

Caitlin slowed and turned around. "Come on!" she urged us. "We don't have much time! We have to find Princess!"

The three of us walked quickly, every few moments stopping to listen to the barking dog. It sounded like we were getting closer, but I couldn't be sure.

But then:

The dog began growling and snarling viciously. The closer we came, the more ferocious the dog sounded.

Caitlin stopped walking.

"Princess?" she called out. We could hear the dog snarling and barking, but we couldn't see her.

And suddenly, a form appeared in the mist.

But it wasn't a dog.

It wasn't Amanda.

It wasn't a shark or a panther.

It was the last thing in the world I wanted to see.

It was the old man.

The old man was grinning his nasty, toothy grin as he walked toward us.

"Ah, yessssss," he began. *"Our lovely children. And how are you doing?"*

"We'll be doing fine, just as soon as we get away from you," Caitlin snapped.

The old man pretended to have his feelings hurt. His smile went away and he cocked his head to one side.

"*Oh, so sad, so sad,*" he said. "*I don't like it when my guests leave so soon. Are you sure you don't want to stay for a while? Maybe just for . . . ever?*"

He laughed a terrible, wicked laugh. It echoed through the fog and all around. I could hear Princess growling and snarling, meaner than ever, but I couldn't see her.

"We're getting Caitlin's dog and we're getting out of here!" I insisted.

The old man raised his eyebrows and took a step toward us. Likewise, Caitlin, Maria and I took a step back. We knew all too well what would happen if we even *touched* the old man.

We'd be trapped in the fog forever.

"*Now, now,*" the old man drawled. "*It's not so bad here. It's really not. Why . . . I kind of like it here. And I think that you will, too. I think all three of you will like your new home.*"

"This isn't our home, you big meany!" Maria burst out.

"*Oh, but it is, child, it is. And you'll have lots of fun here, too. Lots of fun. Why, there are even animals to play with. Do you like animals?*"

136

We didn't answer him. In the fog, we could hear Princess continue to howl and bark.

"Yes, lots of animal friends. As a matter of fact, I have made a new animal friend. Would you like to meet my new animal friend?"

Horror rose up inside of me. I knew that Caitlin was feeling it, too, because we both knew what the old man was getting at.

"Yesssss," he hissed. *"My new dog is such a good, good friend. Of course, we don't know each other very well . . . but we'll be spending a lot of time together. A lot of time, indeed."*

In the mist, another form began to take shape. I heard barking and growling as the creature drew closer.

And in the next instant, my worst fears were confirmed.

It was a dog.

Princess.

But, sadly, the dog was no longer the dog we knew her to be. She had wisping white fur and a creamy gray body.

A wave of sadness fell over me. I felt sick, like I was going to barf right then and there.

Oh no, I thought. *It can't be. It just can't be.*

Princess had come in contact with the old man, and now she was just like him: a phantom of the fog.

This was a nightmare beyond belief. Princess had become a creature of the fog, and there was nothing we could do about it.

But Caitlin was going to try. She suddenly leapt forward, charging at the old man!

"Caitlin! No!" I screamed, but she ignored me! I let go of Maria's hand and raced after Caitlin.

"I'm going to get you for this!" she screamed

at the old man. "I'm going to make you pay for what you did to my dog!"

What did she think she was doing?!?! If she touched the old man, she would become just like Princess! Just like Amanda and the old man and all the other creatures trapped in the fog!

"Caitlin! STOP!" I cried. *"That's what he wants you to do! He wants you to touch him! Then you'll be here forever, too!"*

I was running as fast as I could now, racing after Caitlin. I had to stop her before she reached the old man.

Suddenly, Princess sprang into action. The dog bounded through the fog . . . charging directly at Caitlin!

Caitlin slowed for an instant, and it was the chance I needed.

I was still running like crazy, and I leapt as hard as I could, flying through the air . . . and right on top of Caitlin!

The impact sent her tumbling to the ground. Instantly, I rolled sideways and sprang to my feet.

"Caitlin!" I cried. *"You can't! Remember: if you touch any creature in the fog, you'll become one*

yourself!"

The old man wasn't far away, and he began walking toward us.

"Yesssssss, children," he said, extending a bony hand. *"Stay with me. Stay with me . . . forever."*

Caitlin suddenly leapt to her feet. I grabbed her hand and pulled her away.

"Maria! I shouted. "Where are you!?!?"

"Here I am!" came Maria's high-pitched voice. "Right here!"

Thankfully, she had remained right where I had left her, and we found her easily.

But the old man was coming. He was coming toward us . . . and he was more than just angry.

He was *steaming*. His eyes were filled with hatred and rage.

"The games are over," he sneered. *"I tried to be nice. Well, no more. Now, we'll do this my way!"*

And without any warning, the old man suddenly rose up into the air! He floated like a balloon, arms outstretched, his wiry arms reaching for us!

It was all over. There wasn't anywhere to run, even if we had the time to do so.

The old man would win. Caitlin, Maria and I would be trapped forever in the mysterious cloud.

We were about to become fog phantoms.

All of a sudden, Princess sprang into action.

She bounded through the mist, running toward us. In seconds, she had placed herself between us and the old man! She began growling and barking and snapping at him.

The old man was still floating, suspended in the fog, but he slowed.

It was the time we needed. The three of us

turned to run.

"There is nowhere you can go!" the old man hissed. Princess continued to bark and growl, keeping the old man away from us.

"Go ahead," the old man squawked angrily. *"There's nowhere you can go! You'll be here forever, I tell you. Forever!!"*

I turned around, and I saw the old man still floating in the air. Beneath him, the dog snarled and snapped. The old man was trying to get around the dog, but he couldn't. Princess, now a part of the fog herself, was able to leap high into the air and prevent the old man from chasing after us.

I was glad we got away . . . but I felt incredibly sad. I knew that Caitlin, did, too.

She would never see Princess again. When the fog lifted, it would carry her dog with it. Princess had saved us. She had saved us, but now she would live forever in the creamy, thick cloud.

After we had traveled some distance, we slowed to a walk. We could no longer hear the old man. Princess's barking had faded away into the mist. The three of us were alone once again, but wary that, at any moment, some other creature might attack us from the fog.

Caitlin didn't speak. Neither did Maria. The three of us just walked in silence, not knowing where we were going. We knew that the fog would be lifting soon.

Maria noticed it first.

"Look!" she cried out, pointing.

We stopped walking.

In front of us, several feet away, was a palm tree.

"It's lifting!" I cried out. "The fog is lifting!"

And it was.

It was getting thinner, even as we watched. Soon, several more trees were visible.

"Over there!" Caitlin said. "It looks like a house!"

I looked where she was pointing, and saw what appeared to be a brick wall and several windows.

"It *is* a house!" I said. "That's Peterson's home! We're only a block away from my house! Come on! We have to go this way! Hurry!"

And with that, we set off toward my house.

Amanda had told us that, once the fog began to lift, there would be no time to waste.

Other objects began to appear. I could see trees, bushes, a fence and a shed. They all looked familiar, and I was so happy that I knew where I was.

Home. We were going to make it.

"Look!" Maria cried, pointing as we ran.

It was our house. It was just barely visible in the rising fog, but there was no mistake.

"We're going to make it!" I shouted. "Just a few more feet! We have to get inside the house and out of the fog before it lifts!"

We were almost to the porch. Without warning, Caitlin suddenly stopped.

"What are you doing?!?!" I asked.

"Wait!" she cried. "Did you hear it?"

I listened. The only thing I could hear was my own heaving breath and the pounding of my heart.

"I don't hear anything," I said. "Come on! The fog is lifting!"

I turned to step up onto the porch and open the back door when Caitlin grabbed my arm.

Maria bounded past both of us, threw open the door, and burst inside. She was safe.

But we were still outside!

"Listen!" Caitlin pleaded. "Just listen for a second!"

And then, I heard it.

Far off, in the fog.

Barking. A dog was barking in the fog.

Princess!

The sound of Princess's bark brought tears to Caitlin's eyes. She knew that she would have to leave the dog in the mist . . . or else be trapped in the fog herself.

"Caitlin," I pleaded. "We have to go inside! *Now!*"

"I just want to see her one last time," Caitlin replied. "I just want to say good-bye."

The barking grew closer, and a form began to take shape. The dog suddenly bounded across the yard . . . *followed by Amanda!*

"You must leave quickly," Amanda said. *"The fog is lifting. There isn't much time."*

"I just wanted to see my dog one last time," Caitlin said, watching the misty dog whirl happily in the fog.

"I beg your pardon?" Amanda said. *"You haven't found your dog?"*

Caitlin pointed at Princess's form as the dog ran about in the mist.

Amanda shook her head. *"That's not your dog,"* she said. *"That's my dog, Punky. Here, boy! Come here, Punky!"*

The dog instantly stopped in its tracks and ran up to Amanda.

She was right! The dog wasn't Princess, after all!

It was Amanda's dog, Punky! She had found her dog!

But, that would mean . . . .

"So, it was your dog?!?! Punky saved us from the old man?" Caitlin asked.

Amanda bobbed her head.

"Well, then, where is—"

Caitlin was interrupted by the sound of another barking dog. All three of us turned in the direction of the sound. Punky's ears flew up, and he began to wag his tail.

Then, the dog sprang. Punky began barking, and ran off into the fog.

Seconds ticked by. We waited.

Suddenly, two forms appeared in the thinning fog. One was Punky, and the other . . . .

Princess!

It was Princess, and she hadn't become a fog phantom, after all!

I don't think I've ever seen Caitlin so happy in my entire life. Princess ran up to her, and Caitlin dropped to her knees and threw her arms around the dog's neck.

"You must go now," Amanda urged. *"The fog is leaving, and I will be leaving with it. If you stay any longer, you will become trapped in the fog forever."*

"Thanks for your help," I said. Caitlin thanked her, too, and we turned to step up onto the porch and get inside before it was too late.

But it wasn't to be.

Suddenly, the old man was there. He had been hiding in the bushes, waiting for his chance.

Now he was standing between us and the door . . . blocking us from entering the house!

"*Now, you will stay here,*" the old man wheezed. "*You will stay with us, forever and ever!*"

I backed away, and so did Caitlin.

"*The fog is lifting!*" Amanda said. "*You must get inside! You must get inside before it's too late!*"

The old man began coming toward us.

"How?!?!" I shouted to Amanda. "He's blocking our way!!"

153

And then:

A miracle.

Maria's face appeared in a window. She was looking out at us.

"Maria!" I screamed. "Open the window! Open the window now!"

She looked at me like she didn't understand.

All the while, the old man kept coming closer and closer, and the fog kept getting thinner and thinner.

"Open the window!" Caitlin and I both screamed.

Suddenly, the window slid sideways. Maria's head peered out.

"Huh?" she said. "I couldn't hear you because the window was closed. What do you want?"

"Leave the window open!" I shouted. "I turned to Caitlin. "You go to the left, and I'll go to the right! The old man can't get *both* of us!"

The old man was still coming toward us.

And then, we got the break we needed.

Amanda's dog, Punky, sprang. He began circling the old man like he had done before. It didn't stop him from coming toward us, but it slowed him down a bit.

It was our only chance.

"Now!" I shouted, and Caitlin and I sprang. Princess followed Caitlin. We split in two different directions. If we moved fast, we could make it around the old man and into the house. Caitlin would be close to the back door, so she could get into the house that way. I would be close to the open window, so I could dive through.

"NEVER!" the old man hissed. "It is too late! You will be here forever!"

He lunged out after me, but I was too quick. His hands missed me by several inches.

That left Caitlin open to make it to the back door. She flew onto the porch and grabbed the door, flinging it open and leaping inside. Princess darted through right behind her.

She had made it. Caitlin was safe. Princess was, too.

For me, however, it wasn't going to be so easy.

I sprang to the open window. Maria was there, and so was Caitlin.

"Behind you!" Caitlin screamed. "He's right

behind you!"

I reached the window and dove headfirst. Caitlin grabbed my waist and tried to pull me through.

*"He's going to get you!"*Maria screamed.

Still struggling to get through the window, I managed a quick glance behind me.

The old man was only inches away! I could see his arms reaching out, his wiry fingers opening and closing, opening and closing.

"Now," he said, his voice hissing like a snake., *"Now, you will be one of us. You will become a creature of the fog."*

He reached out his hand to touch my leg.

It was over. There was nothing I could do. I looked at Caitlin, then at Maria.

"Good-bye," I whispered to them.

34

"You're not going anywhere!" Caitlin screamed. I was still part way through the window, and her arms were wrapped around my waist.

"Maria! Help!" she cried. Maria grabbed my hand and pulled.

Behind me, the old man's hand came down. His hand came down, reaching for my leg, reaching, reaching . . . .

157

— and missed!

Suddenly, my whole body went crashing into the house. The three of us — Caitlin, Maria, and I — tumbled into a pile on the floor.

Instantly, I leapt to my feet and slid the window closed. I didn't know if the old man could get into the house, but I sure wasn't going to take any chances!

The old man was only inches from the window, and he was glaring at us. We backed away from the window and watched as he began to fade away like drifting smoke.

"I'll be back," he wheezed angrily. *"I'll be back for you!"*

And with that, his whole body rose up into the mist.

The old man had vanished.

In the yard, I caught a glimpse of Amanda. She, too, was gently rising up into the air, along with her dog. She was waving at us. I couldn't tell for sure, but it looked like she was smiling.

Seconds later, she had vanished into the sky, caught up in the rising fog.

We stood at the window, watching the murky

cloud rise higher and higher. Things began to look normal. I could see trees and other houses. After several minutes, the fog was gone. The day was cloudy and gray, but the fog . . . and the phantoms within it . . . were gone.

"I'm hungry," Maria said. "I want some Spaghetti-O's."

Sheesh, I thought. *We barely escape with our lives, and all she can think about is food.*

"Well, I'd better get home," Caitlin said. "Mom and Dad are probably wondering where I am."

I was wondering the same thing, too . . . sort of. I was wondering where my mom and dad were.

Had they stayed at Grandma and Grandpa's? What would happen if they, too, had become trapped in the fog?

Were they okay?

I shouldn't have worried. Not long after Caitlin went home, the phone rang.

It was Mom.

"They just got the phones working," she told me. "We're still at Grandma and Grandpa's. Is everything okay there?"

"Yeah, fine," I replied.

"Okay. I just wanted to check. There have been some strange reports on the news."

I paused. *Strange reports?* I thought.

"Like . . . what kind of strange reports?" I asked.

"Oh, people saying that they saw things moving in the fog. Odd things. But you know how people can be, especially after a hurricane.

"Yeah," I agreed, looking out the window.

"I'm glad the fog is gone, though," Mom said.

"I am too," I replied. "I am, too."

I didn't say anything about the phantoms. She wouldn't have believed me, anyway.

And I kept wondering what that old man had told me. He said that he would be back. He had said that he was going to return, and the way he had said it chilled me to the bone.

No, I thought. *He's gone. He left with the fog. He can't get me now. I'll never see him again.*

At least, that's what I told myself.

That night, I would discover that I was wrong.

Mom and Dad came home later that day. I was going to go for a bike ride when Mom stopped me in the hall.

"What have you been telling your little sister?" she asked me. Her voice was stern.

"What do you mean?"

"She says that you and Caitlin got lost in the fog. She says that there were things chasing you."

And so . . . I told her the truth. I told her about everything. About the fog phantoms, the shark, the panther and the whale. I told her about Amanda and the old man, and the Portuguese man-o-war.

Mom listened intently, patiently. When I was finished, she smiled.

"That's a great story," she said, "but I don't want you telling Maria things like that. She'll have nightmares."

"But . . . but it really happened," I said. "It really, really did."

Mom shook her head. "With ideas like that, I think you'd be a very good writer. You should write that down and make it into a story."

And with that, she strode off. I could have argued all day with her, and she still wouldn't believe that I had been telling her the truth.

And maybe it was better that way.

That night, I had a dream about the old man. I dreamed that I had been walking home from school. The day was really foggy.

And the old man was there. He appeared from nowhere, reaching out with his bony fingers.

"*I told you I'd be back,*" he was saying. "*I told you. Now, you're coming with ME!*"

He reached out and touched my arm . . . and that's when I woke up. I was in my bed.

It had only been a dream.

Outside, the glow of the streetlight lit up my bedroom.

But there was no fog. I could see shapes and shadows, and even Caitlin's house across the street.

No fog.

Whew.

I rolled over in bed, and when I saw the white, wispy shape of the old man standing in the door of my bedroom, I screamed and screamed and screamed.

"What on earth are you shouting about?"

A light clicked on, and I squinted.

It was Dad! He was wearing his white pajamas, and in the dim glow of the outside streetlight, I had thought that he was the old man!

"Oh, man!" I exclaimed. "Am I glad it's just you!"

"Who did you think it was?" he asked.

165

"I thought that it was . . . oh, I was just having a nightmare."

"I'm not surprised," Dad said, "after the story you made up today. You've got quite an imagination."

Imagination nothing, I thought. *That stuff really happened.*

Dad returned to bed, and, after a while, I fell back to sleep.

The next day was sunny and bright. And hot, too. Florida gets some really hot weather . . . especially in the summer. My friends and I go to the beach a lot. We don't live too far from the ocean, and it's a lot of fun. We swim and snorkel and play beach games.

I called Caitlin to see if she wanted to go to the beach.

"Sounds cool," she said. I went over to her house, and we rode our bikes down to a nearby park. We met up with a lot of other friends, too. Seems like everyone was at the beach that day.

Later in the afternoon, we chose sides for a game of beach volleyball. Two kids that I didn't know came up to ask if they could play.

"Sure," I said. "The more, the merrier. I'm Justin," I said to the one with dark hair. He was a little taller than me, and I was glad to have him on our team.

"I'm Mike, and this is my brother, Brad."

"Come on," I said. "The game's about to start."

And Mike and Brad were pretty good players, too. We won all three games that we played.

Afterwards, we sat at a picnic table in the shade. I offered my new friends some cold juice, and they sat down at the table. Caitlin grabbed a juice for herself from the cooler and sat down next to me.

"Where are you guys from?" Caitlin asked.

"New York, Brad replied. He sipped his juice. "We live in Albany, in upstate New York."

"Wow," I said. "Are you here on vacation?"

"Yeah," Mike replied. Then he looked at Brad and laughed. But I sensed fear in his voice, too. "We came here to vacation, and to stay away from the ninjas," he said.

Caitlin giggled, but I saw the look on Mike's

face. He was serious.

"What do you mean, 'ninjas'?" I asked.

Mike looked at Brad. He leaned over and whispered something. Brad nodded.

"Can you keep a secret?" he asked.

"Sure," I answered, and Caitlin nodded.

"Well, we'll tell you, then," Brad said.

And when they finished their story, Caitlin and I just sat there in disbelief.

What Mike and Brad had told us was freaky. *Far* freakier than any phantoms in the fog, that's for sure . . . .

next in the

AMERICAN CHILLERS

series:

#4:

NEW YORK

NINJAS

turn the page to read a few spine-chilling chapters . . . if you dare!

1

There are some things in this world that you just can't explain, no matter how hard you try.

This is one of those stories.

It happened to me and my friends last fall, and to make things even creepier, it happened on the scariest day of the year.

October 31st.

Halloween.

It was Friday, and I was in my bedroom doing my homework when my brother, Brad, suddenly jumped into the doorway. He was dressed in a ghost costume. I have to admit, he surprised me a little, but I wasn't about to let him know.

"Hahahaha! Gotcha!" he laughed, his arms raised up in the air. His costume was only an old sheet with holes where his eyes were.

I shook my head. "You didn't get me at all," I said. "You look like a skinny marshmallow."

He dropped his arms. I could see his eyes staring at me through the torn holes in the sheet.

"Come on, Mike," he said to me. "Why don't you just bag that stuff until Sunday?" he said, pointing at my homework on my desk.

I shook my head. "I'm going to get it done now so I don't have to worry about it all weekend," I replied.

He shrugged and left, and I returned to my homework.

That's where Brad and I are different. I'm twelve, and one year older than he is. I like to take care of things and make sure that they're done right.

Brad, on the other hand, is a little more carefree. Oh, don't get me wrong. He's no doofus. He just likes to have his fun.

I guess we all do, now and then.

And I have to admit, I was really excited about that night.

Halloween.

My brother and I, along with Sarah Wheeler, were going to go trick-or-treating. Sarah and her family just moved into the house across the street. We live in Albany, New York, which is about one hundred and fifty miles north of New York City. That's where Sarah and her family moved from. She's pretty cool, and the three of us had been hanging out together.

After trick-or-treating, we were all going to go to the big Halloween party in the school gym.

We would never make it.

In just a few short hours, we would be running down sidewalks, house to house, ringing doorbells and knocking on doors.

The usual Halloween stuff.

Only, tonight would be different.

Tonight wouldn't go as planned.

Tonight, Brad, Sarah and I would find something that would lead to the scariest night of our lives.

I had just finished my homework when I heard the doorbell ring. I heard Brad talking in the living room, and then I heard Sarah's giggle. I'd know her laugh anywhere. Sarah is the same age as Brad, only she's a little taller. And they both have the same black hair, except Sarah wears hers a lot longer.

In the next instant, there was a ghost and a witch standing at the door of my bedroom.

"Hey!" I exclaimed, admiring Sarah's costume. "That looks great!"

Her eyes grew wide, and she let out with a sharp cackle. It was funny, and we all laughed.

"You're not even in costume?!?!" Sarah said. "It's almost six o'clock!"

"He's been doing his homework," Brad sneered from beneath the white sheet.

"It'll take me ten minutes," I said. "You guys go down to the park and I'll meet you there."

They left, and I put my homework into my folder and slid it under my bed.

Then I put my costume on. This year, I was a vampire. I made the costume myself, using one of Mom's old tablecloths as a cape. I bought a cheap Halloween make-up kit at the department store, and I made my face all white, with dark, shadowy circles around my eyes. I slicked my hair back with gel, then I stared in the mirror and smiled. I really did look pretty scary.

Cool.

Minutes later, I met up with Brad and Sarah at the park.

"Mike, you look *awesome!*" Sarah shouted as I approached.

"I vant to drink your blood!" I said, wrapping

my hands gently around her neck. Sarah laughed and drew away.

"Come on," Brad said from beneath the white sheet. "There are people already trick-or-treating!"

We started out. The evening sun had fallen below the trees, but it was still light out. The night was warm, too, for which I was thankful. October can be chilly in Albany, and I didn't want to have to wear a coat over my costume.

There were a lot of other kids trick or treating. I'm sure I knew most of them, but it was hard to recognize anyone in their costume.

We had just rounded the block, when all of a sudden a dark form came from around the bushes at the corner. I tried to get out of the way—but it was too late!

The figure slammed into me, and I was sent sprawling into the bushes. Branches scratched my face, and my bag of candy went flying. I heard Sarah scream. Brad gasped.

"Hey!" Sarah shouted angrily. "Why don't you watch where you're going!?!?"

"Mike!" Brad said, scrambling to help me. I

was still tangled up in the thick brush. "Are you okay?!?!"

But I wasn't paying any attention. In fact, I barely even heard him talking to me.

My attention was focused on what was partially buried beneath the dead leaves on the ground. I struggled to pull the branches away, then I swept the brittle, brown leaves aside. Now I could see the entire object.

My eyes grew.

My heart drummed.

Time stopped.

"Wow," I whispered beneath my breath.

What I had found was *incredible*.

A mask.

That's what was buried within the leaves.

But it wasn't just *any* mask. At least, it sure didn't look like any ordinary costume mask.

"Mike? Are you all right?" I heard Sarah ask. I felt a hand grasp my foot, and someone started to pull me out of the bushes.

"Hang on a second!" I said excitedly. "I found something!"

"Yeah," Brad sneered. "You found a bush. You fell into it when a big kid bumped into you."

I ignored him.

The mask was dirty and stained from being in the weather. I picked it up, then struggled out of the bushes, without help from my brother.

"Check this out!" I said, scrambling to my feet. I held the mask up for Brad and Sarah to see.

"That's cool," Sarah said.

"What is it?" Brad asked.

"It's a Japanese Kabuki mask," I replied.

"A *what?*" Brad asked.

"A Japanese Kabuki mask," I repeated. "And it's old. It must have been in those bushes for a long time."

"How do *you* know what it is?" he asked. I could tell he thought that I was making it up.

"Because I'm older and smarter than you, that's why," I replied.

I wiped some of the dirt away from the mask. It was a reddish-gold color, but it had faded with age. The mask was heavy, and appeared to be made out of wood or some other thick material. It sure wasn't made of cheap plastic like those masks you buy at the store!

"Let me see," Sarah said.

I handed her the mask, and she held it up.

"This is cool," she said.

"Is it part of someone's Halloween costume?" Brad asked. He reached out with his ghostly arms. Sarah handed the mask to him.

"No," I replied. "Kabuki is an old form of Japanese theater. The performers use masks like these."

"I'll bet I could scare some kids with this thing!" Brad said, holding the mask up to his sheet-covered face.

"Brad, don't do that," Sarah said sharply.

"Why? Are you afraid of what I'll look like?"

"Give it back to me," I ordered, reaching out to take the mask away.

Suddenly, Brad placed the mask over his face.

"Ha ha ha!" he said, his voice muffled. "Ka-BOOOO-keee!" He held the mask to his face with one hand, then raised his free arm. "Get it? Ka-BOOOOOO-keeeeeeee!"

"Stop being a goofball!" I ordered. "Give me the mask. I'm the one who found it!"

"Ka-BOOOOO-keeeeee!" Brad repeated.

"Brad! Stop it!" Sarah said.

"Why?" Brad asked. "Am I scaring you?" He placed both hands on the side of the mask.

"What the . . . ?" he said. There was a hint of panic in his voice.

"Hey!" he shouted. He was gripping the mask, trying to pry it from his face. "It's . . . it's got me! I . . . I can't get it off!"

And then he began to scream.

Brad started whirling, spinning around, his face grasping the mask!

"It won't come off!" he shrieked. "It . . . it won't come off!"

Sarah and I rushed to help.

"Brad! Stop!" Sarah cried. "Stop! We can help!"

Brad continued clawing at the mask over his face. Then he suddenly dove to the ground and began rolling in the grass.

"Brad!" I ordered. "Stop moving!"

In the next instant, Brad bounced back up to his feet. He had both hands on the mask, and he slowly pulled it away.

"Ha ha ha!" he snickered. "Gotcha!"

"You creep!" Sarah scolded. "You scared me!"

I snatched the mask from his hands.

"You don't know what you're doing," I said angrily. "This thing might be worth a lot of money."

"It's just a silly old mask," Brad said. "Besides — it's pretty dirty. Whoever it belongs to probably gave up looking for it before I was even born."

Brad was right. Whoever had owned the mask had probably forgotten about it long ago.

"I still think it's kind of cool," I said, handing the mask to Sarah. She held it while I picked up my bag and gathered up my Halloween candy that had spilled when I fell. Then I took the mask and gently placed it into my bag.

"Come on," Brad said, staring up into the sky. "It'll be dark soon. I want to hit the next block of houses before we call it a night."

"And the Halloween party at the school will be starting soon, too," Sarah said. "We'd better finish up our trick-or-treating or we're going to be late."

We set off, a ghost, a witch, and a vampire, bouncing from house to house, filling our bags with delicious Halloween candy and chocolate and caramel apples and other tasty treats.

Darkness seemed to come quickly that night, and soon, we were just three shadows beneath the glow of the streetlights.

Of course, we had no way of knowing it at the time, but as we made our way down the last row of houses, as we walked along the sidewalk carrying our bags of Halloween candy—

— *we were being followed!*

Sarah sensed it first.

We were just about ready to knock on the door of the last house on the street. Then, we were going to drop our candy off at our house and head for the school.

Just before I rang the doorbell, Sarah spun around.

I held my finger to the button, but I didn't press it.

"What's the matter?" I asked. Sarah was looking into the shadows on the other side of the street.

"Oh, I don't know," she replied. "I just had a funny feeling, that's all. It's probably nothing."

I stared across the street. Windows in houses glowed yellow. Spiny, leafless trees fingered up into the dark night. Bushes cast spooky shadows over lawns and driveways. There were no sounds at all.

And everything seemed oddly still. There were no other trick-or-treaters, no other people outside. It was as if, for the moment, the entire city had stopped.

I was about to ring the doorbell when I heard a noise next door. It sounded like crunching leaves and branches. Brad and Sarah heard the noise, too. We all turned and peered into the bushes in the next yard.

All we could see were shadows.

"Who's there?" Brad called out.

There was no reply.

A gentle, cold breeze suddenly slithered against my cheek. A chill swept through my body, and Sarah's witch hat fell off before she could grab it. Her hair swished in the wind.

As she reached to the ground to pick up her hat, we heard the noise again.

Crunch. Ker-crunch.

We froze.

Sarah remained kneeling. Her hands grasped her hat, but she was staring off into the darkness.

"Who's there?" I demanded. "Stop trying to scare us."

"Yeah," Brad chimed in. "Come out where we can see you."

I figured that it was probably some kid hiding in the bushes. There was someone—or maybe a couple of people—hiding in the bushes, waiting to jump out and scare us.

After all . . . it was Halloween. That's what you do on Halloween. You try to give someone a scare.

Suddenly, the noise came again, except it was much closer now. Sarah stood up and took a step away from the bush.

Whatever it was, it was in the thick shrubbery next to the porch.

Right next to us.

"All right," I said, bravely stepping forward.

"Knock it off, whoever you are."

I reached out to grab a branch. I was planning on pulling the branches away to find out who was hiding.

That's what I was planning, anyway.

But that's not what happened.

Because the instant I grabbed the branch was the instant that I saw the sinister, glowing eyes, glaring back at me from within the bush.

And I knew one thing for sure:

The eyes didn't belong to any prankster. They didn't belong to any costumed trick-or-treater.

Whatever was in the bushes wasn't human!

And suddenly, the creature lunged . . . and came straight at us!

VISIT:

WWW.AMERICANCHILLERS.COM

to find out more about this exciting NEW book series from Johnathan Rand! Read sample stories for FREE, and join the official American Chillers Fan Club! Plus, check out Mr. Rand's on-line journal, featuring pictures and stories during his journeys! It's like traveling with him yourself! You'll get the inside scoop on when and where he'll be, and what projects he's working on right now!

About the author

Johnathan Rand is the author of the best-selling **'Chillers'** series, now with over 1,000,000 copies in print. In addition to the **'Chillers'** series, Rand is also the author of **'Ghost in the Graveyard',** a collection of thrilling, original   short stories featuring *The Adventure Club.* (And don't forget to check out **www.ghostinthegraveyard.com** and read an **entire story** from 'Ghost in the Graveyard' *FREE!*) When Mr. Rand and his wife are not traveling to schools and book signings, they live in a small town in northern lower Michigan with their two dogs, Abby and Salty. He still writes all of his books in the wee hours of the morning, and still submits all manuscripts by mail. He is currently working on his newest series, entitled **'American Chillers'**. His popular website features hundreds of photographs, stories, and art work. Visit:

WWW.AMERICANCHILLERS.COM

Also by Johnathan Rand:

193

FUN FACTS ABOUT FLORIDA:

State Capitol: Tallahassee

Became a state in 1845

27th state in the Union

State Bird: Mockingbird

State Animal: Panther

State Tree: Sabal Palm

Named by Ponce De Leon on Easter in 1513 - 'Pascua Florida' means 'Flowery Easter'.

State Flower: Orange Blossom

State Nickname: The Sunshine State

The state of Florida encompasses 54,252 square miles

SOME FAMOUS PEOPLE FROM FLORIDA

☞ **Osceola,** Seminole Indian leader

☞ **Charles and John Ringling,** co-founders of Ringling Bros. and Barnum & Bailey Circus

☞ **Janet Reno,** first woman attorney general of the US; born in Miami

☞ **Sidney Poitier,** first African-American to win an Oscar; born in Miami

☞ **Wallace Amos,** founder of 'Famous Amos' Chocolate Chip Cookie Corporation

☞ **David Robinson,** basketball player, born in Key West

*Other famous people from Florida include singer/songwriter **Gloria Estefan,** baseball player **Dwight Gooden,** singer **Jim Morrison** of **The Doors,** baseball player **Steve 'Lefty' Carlton,** airplane pilot **Jacqueline Cochran,** dancer **Fernando Bujones,** singer **Pat Boone,** actor **Ben Vereen,** actress **Faye Dunaway,** jazz saxophonist **Julian Cannonball Adderley,** among many others!*

AMERICAN CHILLERS
PICTURE PAGES!

Chiller fans!

AMERICAN CHILLERS
PICTURE PAGES!

Johnathan & Mrs. Rand, arriving in style for a book
signing at Barnes & Noble, Saginaw, Michigan!

AMERICAN CHILLERS
PICTURE PAGES!

With Debra Gantz at Hickory Woods Elementary!

AMERICAN CHILLERS
PICTURE PAGES!

Getting out the scare at Ann Arbor Public Library!

AMERICAN CHILLERS
PICTURE PAGES!

Chilling out at Pattengill Elementary!

AMERICAN CHILLERS
PICTURE PAGES!

A sellout performance at Roseville Public Library!

AMERICAN CHILLERS
PICTURE PAGES!

A warm welcome at Eastlawn Elementary!

For information on personal appearances, motivational speaking engagements, or book signings, write to:

AudioCraft Publishing, Inc.
PO Box 281
Topinabee Island, MI 49791

or call
(231) 238-4424

Now available! Official 'Michigan
& American Chillers' Wearables,
including:

-Embroidered hats
-Embroidered T-Shirts

Visit www.americanchillers.com to
order yours!

Join the official

AMERICAN CHILLERS

FAN CLUB!

Visit www.americanchillers.com for details

About the cover art: This unique cover was designed and created by Michigan artists Darrin Brege and Mark Thompson.

Darrin Brege works as an animator by day, and is now applying his talents on the internet, creating various web sites and flash animations. He attended animation school in southern California in the early nineties, and over the years has created original characters and animations for Warner Bros (Space Jam), for Hasbro (Tonka Joe Multimedia line), Universal Pictures (Bullwinkle and Fractured Fairy Tales CD Roms), and Disney. Besides art, he and his wife Karen are improv performers featured weekly at Mark Ridley's Comedy Castle over the last eight years. Improvisational comedy has provided the groundwork for a successful voice over career as well. Darrin has dozens of characters and impersonations in his portfolio. Darrin and Karen have a son named Mick.

Mark Thompson has been a professional illustrator for 25 years. He has applied his talents with toy companies Hasbro and Mattel, along with creating art for automobile companies. His work has been seen from San Diego Seaworld to Kmart stores, as well as the Detroit Tigers and the renowned 'Screams' ice-cream parlor in Hell, Michigan. Mark currently is designing holiday crafts for a local company, as well as doing website design and digital art from his home studio. He loves sci-fi and monster art, and also collects comics for a hobby. He has two boys of his own, and they're BIG Chiller Fans!

All AudioCraft books are proudly printed, bound, and manufactured in the United States of America, utilizing American resources, labor, and materials.

USA